This Ladybird Book belongs to:

Kate

Read together books are designed for you and your child to share.

There was an old woman has a text for children to read, and an adult text that tells the rhyme and asks questions. These will encourage your child to think about the rhyme and to look more closely at the pictures.

First, read the book aloud. Then go through the story again, this time allowing your child to 'read' the text. The illustrations give clues to the words. Many young children will remember the words rather than be able to read them, but this is a normal part of pre-reading. Always praise as you go along – keep your reading sessions fun and stop if your child loses interest.

Ladybird books are widely available, but in case of difficulty may be ordered by post or telephone from:

Ladybird Books – Cash Sales Department
Littlegate Road Paignton Devon TQ3 3BE
Telephone 0803 554761

A catalogue record for this book is available from the British Library

Published by Ladybird Books Ltd Loughborough Leicestershire UK
Ladybird Books Inc Auburn Maine 04210 USA

Printed in EC

There was an old woman

by Hy Murdock

illustrated by Terry Burton

This old woman is in her garden.

How many animals can you see in the picture?

There was an old woman
who swallowed a fly.
I don't know why she swallowed a fly.
Perhaps she'll die.

Here is a fly.

How many wings does the fly have?

There was an old woman
who swallowed a spider
That wriggled and jiggled and
tickled inside her.

This is a spider.

Count the spider's legs.

She swallowed the spider to catch the fly.
I don't know why she swallowed a fly.
Perhaps she'll die.

The old woman
is laughing.

*Are you
ticklish?*

There was an old woman
who swallowed a bird.
How absurd, to swallow a bird!

There are some birds
in this tree.

Which bird is singing?

There was an old woman
who swallowed a cat.
Well fancy that, she swallowed a cat!

Here is a cat with her kittens.

Do you like milk?

The old woman
swallowed the fly.

The spider chased
the fly.

The bird chased
the spider.

The cat chased
the bird.

There was an old woman
who swallowed a dog.
What a hog, to swallow a dog!

Here are some dogs.
They are playing.

Which dog is brown and white?

There was an old woman
who swallowed a cow.
I don't know how she swallowed a cow!

There are five cows in the field.

How many cows are lying down?

She swallowed the cow to catch the dog.
She swallowed the dog to catch the cat.
She swallowed the cat to catch the bird.
She swallowed the bird to catch the spider.
She swallowed the spider to catch the fly.

Look at the animals.

Which animals did the old woman swallow?

There was an old woman
who swallowed a horse.

She's dead of course!

The rhyme

There was an old woman who swallowed a fly.
I don't know why she swallowed a fly.
Perhaps she'll die.

There was an old woman who swallowed a spider
That wriggled and jiggled and tickled inside her.
She swallowed the spider to catch the fly.
I don't know why she swallowed a fly.
Perhaps she'll die.

There was an old woman who swallowed a bird.
How absurd, to swallow a bird!
She swallowed the bird to catch the spider… etc.

There was an old woman who swallowed a cat.
Well fancy that, she swallowed a cat!
She swallowed the cat to catch the bird… etc.

There was an old woman who swallowed a dog.
What a hog, to swallow a dog!
She swallowed the dog to catch the cat... etc.

There was an old woman who swallowed a cow.
I don't know how she swallowed a cow!
She swallowed the cow to catch the dog.
She swallowed the dog to catch the cat.
She swallowed the cat to catch the bird.
She swallowed the bird to catch the spider
That wriggled and jiggled and tickled inside her.
She swallowed the spider to catch the fly.
I don't know why she swallowed a fly.
Perhaps she'll die.

There was an old woman who swallowed a horse.
She's dead of course!